AHILYABAI HOLKAR

IT WAS THE YEAR 1733 A.D. MALHARRAO HOLKAR AND HIS MEN WERE ON THEIR WAY HOME FROM A TOUR OF THE COUNTRY. THEY DECIDED TO HALT FOR THE NIGHT AT A TEMPLE IN CHOUNDI VILLAGE NEAR AURANGABAD. AS THEY STOOD IN THE COURTYARD WITH THE VILLAGERS WHO HAD GATHERED FOR THE EVENING PRAYERS, A LITTLE GIRL ENTERED.

ALL EYES TURNED TOWARDS HER.

BUT SHE WAS OBLIVIOUS OF THEM.

SHE PAID OBEISANCE TO THE IDOL.

2

MALHARRAO WAS SPELLBOUND WITH ADMIRATION.

HOW DEVOUT! WHAT MODESTY! SUCH ARISTOCRATIC MANNERS AND BEARING!

THE PRAYER CAME TO AN END.

MALHARRAO MADE A DECISION.

SHE SHALL BECOME MY DAUGHTER-IN-LAW, WHOEVER SHE MAY BE. IN ALL THE COUNTRY I HAVE NOT COME ACROSS ONE LIKE HER. SHE IS THE WIFE MY WAYWARD SON KHANDERAO NEEDS.

HE TURNED TO ONE OF THE VILLAGERS—

WHO IS THAT CHILD?

SHE IS AHILYA, THE EIGHT-YEAR-OLD DAUGHTER OF OUR PATIL, MANKOJI SHINDE.

NOT WILLING TO WASTE A MOMENT, HE APPROACHED MANKOJI AND SECURED HIS ASSENT.

WHEN SHALL WE ARRANGE THE WEDDING?

THE ALMANAC SHOWS THE FOURTEENTH DAY OF MAY TO BE THE MOST AUSPICIOUS.

SO ON MAY 14, 1733 AHILYABAI WAS MARRIED TO KHANDERAO.

SOON AFTER THE CEREMONY—

GO MY CHILD, WITH MY BLESSINGS! MAY BOTH FAMILIES BE PROUD OF YOU!

THE MOMENT AHILYA STARTED LIFE IN HER NEW HOME AT INDORE SHE REALISED THAT KHANDERAO WAS NOT THE BEST OF SONS OR HUSBANDS.

BUT I SHOULD NOT LET THAT AFFECT MY REGARD FOR HIM. I AM SURE THAT WITH PATIENCE AND UNDERSTANDING HE'LL CHANGE.

SHE SOON BECAME A FAVOURITE WITH HER MOTHER-IN-LAW, GAUTAMABAI.

IT WAS A LUCKY DAY FOR US WHEN YOU DECIDED TO HALT AT CHOUNDI. AHILYA'S DILIGENCE IN HOUSEHOLD MATTERS IS UNMATCHED.

YES! SHE IS AN EXTRAORDINARY GIRL. I HAVE DECIDED TO TRAIN HER IN WARFARE AND STATECRAFT.

AHILYA WAS CAREFUL NOT TO LET HER LEARNING ESTRANGE HER FROM HER HUSBAND. INSTEAD —

I MUST REPEAT ALL THAT I LEARN EACH DAY TO MY HUSBAND.

APART FROM THAT SHE OFTEN TOLD HIM STORIES FROM THE EPICS AND GENTLY INFLUENCED HIS THINKING.

AND WITH HER PATIENCE SHE SOON BROUGHT ABOUT A CHANGE IN KHANDERAO.

AHILYA HAS SUCCEEDED WHERE I HAD FAILED. KHANDERAO HAS ACTUALLY EXPRESSED A WISH TO JOIN ME IN MY CAMPAIGNS.

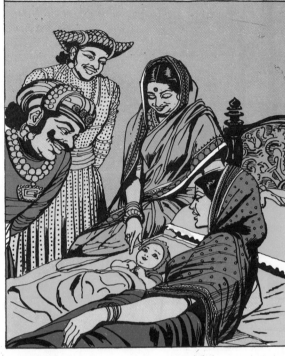

THEN IN 1745 A SON, MALERAO, WAS BORN TO THEM...

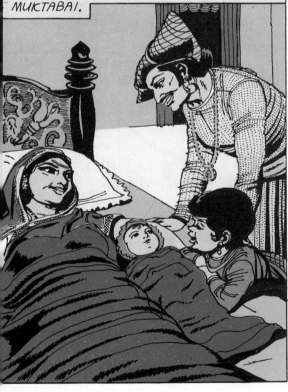

...AND THREE YEARS LATER A DAUGHTER, MUKTABAI.

AS THE DAYS PASSED MALHARRAO'S AFFECTION AND RESPECT FOR AHILYABAI INCREASED.

FROM THE DAY SHE STEPPED INTO OUR HOUSEHOLD BOTH, MY KINGDOM AND I HAVE PROSPERED.

AHILYA HAD BEEN QUICK TO ABSORB ALL THAT MALHARRAO TAUGHT HER.

AT LAST I CAN GO AWAY ON MY CAMPAIGNS WITH AN EASY MIND. I KNOW AHILYA CAN MANAGE THE KINGDOM WHEN I AM AWAY.

WHEN MALHARRAO WAS AWAY AHILYA RULED THE KINGDOM FOR HIM. SHE TOURED THE CITY TO SEE THAT THE PEOPLE WERE CONTENT.

SHE GAVE EAR TO THE LEAST OF COMPLAINTS.

SHE WAS KIND AND HELPFUL TO ALL.

DEVIJI, THERE IS A MAN WHO IS ON HIS WAY TO BANARAS. HE WANTS TO KNOW WHICH ROAD HE SHOULD TAKE.

DRAW A ROAD MAP FOR HIM FROM HERE TO BANARAS. AND... SEE THAT HE HAS SUFFICIENT FOOD FOR THE WAY.

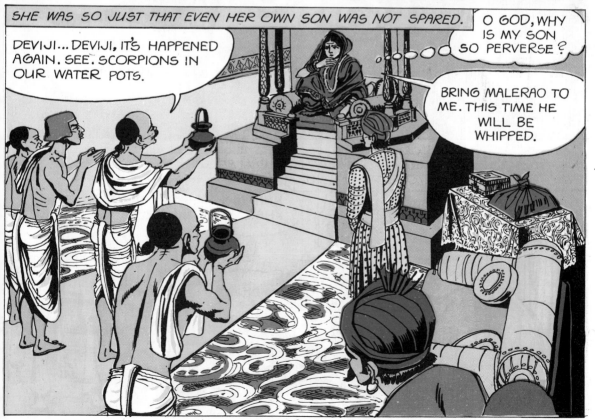

SHE WAS SO JUST THAT EVEN HER OWN SON WAS NOT SPARED.

DEVIJI... DEVIJI, IT'S HAPPENED AGAIN. SEE. SCORPIONS IN OUR WATER POTS.

O GOD, WHY IS MY SON SO PERVERSE?

BRING MALERAO TO ME. THIS TIME HE WILL BE WHIPPED.

AHILYA OFTEN JOINED MALHARRAO AND KHANDERAO ON EXPEDITIONS. ONCE WHILE THEY WERE LAYING SIEGE TO SURAJMAL JAT AT FORT KHUMBERI ALONG WITH RAGHOBA, MADHAVRAO PESHWA'S UNCLE—

HOW PROUD I AM OF KHANDERAO — HE IS NOW A FIT SUCCESSOR. AND ALL BECAUSE OF AHILYA...

HIS THOUGHTS WERE RUDELY DISTURBED BY A BULLET SHOT AND SCREAMS.

THEY'RE FIRING FROM THE FORT.

KHANDERAO...!

HE'S DEAD.

KILLED BY THE BULLET.

MALHARRAO LOST CONTROL OVER HIMSELF. HE RAN BERSERK — RAGHOBA AND OTHER SARDARS TRIED TO RESTRAIN HIM.

KHANDU, KHANDU...

AHILYA CAME RUNNING FROM THE OPPOSITE DIRECTION.

WHY HAVE YOU LEFT ME? WHAT IS LIFE TO ME NOW? FOR WHOM SHOULD I LIVE?

WHEN HE SAW AHILYA BREAK DOWN, MALHARRAO CONTROLLED HIS OWN GRIEF. HE TRIED TO CONSOLE HIS DAUGHTER-IN-LAW AS SHE CRIED HER HEART OUT.

WHEN SHE HAD CALMED DOWN—

I MUST PREPARE MYSELF FOR SATI. I SHALL JOIN HIM.

NO! NEVER! AHILYA WHAT...

11

AHILYA LOOKED UP AT HIM.

YOU CANNOT LEAVE ME ALONE. TAKE PITY ON THIS OLD MAN.

SHE WAS MOVED. SHE ARGUED WITH HERSELF FOR A LONG WHILE.

I HAVE SELFISHLY DWELT ON MY OWN AGONY. MY FATHER-IN-LAW IS OLD; MY CHILDREN YOUNG. THEY NEED ME. IF I PERFORM SATI IT WOULD BE FOR MY SELFISH ENDS — MY OWN SALVATION. BUT IF I LIVE, I CAN BE A SOURCE OF STRENGTH NOT ONLY TO MY OWN FAMILY BUT TO THE PEOPLE.

FATHER, I HAVE DECIDED NOT TO PERFORM SATI. I SHALL LIVE FOR THE SERVICE OF OTHERS.

I AM GRATEFUL TO YOU, AHILYA. I AM VERY GRATEFUL.

AS MALHARRAO GREW OLDER, HE RELIED MORE AND MORE ON AHILYA.

AHILYA, PROMISE ME THAT WHATEVER HAPPENS, YOU WILL TAKE CARE OF OUR KINGDOM.

I PROMISE, FATHER!

IN 1766 WHEN RAGHOBA, THE PESHWA'S UNCLE, WENT TO REGAIN THE PRESTIGE THEY HAD LOST AT THE BATTLE OF PANIPAT IN 1761, MALHARRAO WENT WITH HIM. MAHADJI SCINDIA OF GWALIOR, TOO, WAS WITH THEM.

AT ALAMPUR, MALHARRAO FELL ILL AND WAS ON HIS DEATH-BED.

MAHADJI, I HAVE ONE LAST REQUEST TO MAKE. SEE THAT MY GRANDSON MALERAO SERVES THE PESHWAS WELL, AFTER ME.

MAHADJI WAS TOUCHED.

AS LONG AS I AM ALIVE, I'LL SEE THAT THE HOLKAR LINE IS UNHARMED.

A FEW HOURS LATER MALHARRAO DIED. WHEN THE NEWS REACHED AHILYA—

WHY WAS I NOT THERE TO SERVE HIM WHEN HIS END CAME?

MALERAO UNFORTUNATELY WAS ABNORMAL. AHILYA WROTE TO HIM AS SOON AS MALHARRAO DIED—

...YOU SHOULD THINK OF YOUR DUTIES AS A CHIEF WHO HAS TO RUN THE GOVERNMENT...

BUT ALL HER EFFORTS WERE OF NO AVAIL. MALERAO WAS MENTALLY A SICK PERSON. AT LAST—

THERE IS NO HOPE.

HIS ILLNESS SAPPED HIS VERY LIFE. AHILYA WAS HEART-BROKEN.

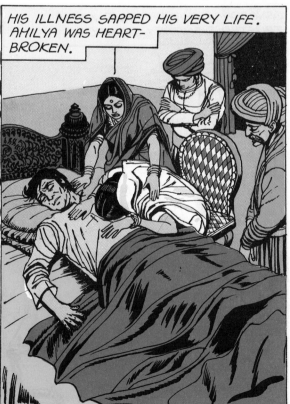

HOW I WISH I COULD GO AWAY TO THE PEACE OF THE HIMALAYAS FOR SOME TIME...BUT NO...

BUT SHE DID NOT HAVE THE TIME EVEN TO GRIEVE FOR HER SON.

SHE WAS SOLELY RESPONSIBLE FOR HER KINGDOM NOW.

"...WHAT WILL MY SUBJECTS DO? I CANNOT AFFORD TO INDULGE IN GRIEF. I HAVE WORK TO DO.

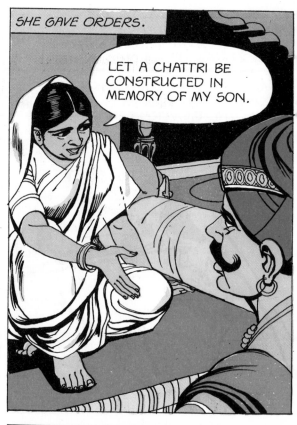

SHE GAVE ORDERS.

LET A CHATTRI BE CONSTRUCTED IN MEMORY OF MY SON.

WHILE AHILYA WAS BUSY BEARING THE BURDEN OF ADMINISTRATION AT INDORE, RAGHOBA, THE PESHWA'S UNCLE, WAS AT UJJAIN.

RAGHOBAJI, HERE IS A PERSONAL MESSAGE FROM GANGADHAR CHANDRACHUD.

GIVE IT TO ME.

GANGADHAR CHANDRACHUD WAS A TRUSTED DIGNITARY OF INDORE.

AHILYABAI WILL NOT MAKE MUKTABAI THE HEIR AS THAT WOULD BE AGAINST OUR RELIGION. THIS IS A GOOD OPPORTUNITY FOR YOU TO SEE THAT THE HOLKAR KINGDOM COMES DIRECTLY UNDER THE PESHWAS. I AM HERE TO OBEY YOUR ORDERS —

RAGHOBA WAS ELATED.

SHABASH, CHANDRACHUD!

HE REPLIED IMMEDIATELY TO CHANDRACHUD'S LETTER.

...OUR HANDS ARE STRENGTHENED BECAUSE OF FAITHFUL SERVANTS LIKE YOU.

AT LAST RAGHOBA'S DREAMS SEEMED TO BE COMING TRUE. HE TURNED TO HIS SARDARS.

GET THE INFANTRY AND CAVALRY READY IMMEDIATELY. I WANT AN ARMY OF 50,000. WE WILL LEAVE TOMORROW NIGHT.

ON TO INDORE —

MEANWHILE IN INDORE—

IT IS HEREBY NOTIFIED BY THIS DECLA-RATION THAT BY THE GRACE OF GOD ALMIGHTY, AHILYABAI HAS ASSUMED ALL POWERS FOR THE KINGDOM OF THE HOLKARS.

THANK THE GOOD GOD. THERE HAS YET TO BE A BETTER AND MORE JUST PERSON THAN HER EVEN THOUGH SHE IS A WOMAN.

DEVIJI, MAY YOU LIVE FOR A THOUSAND YEARS! MAY I HAVE A WORD WITH YOU?

YES. SAY WHAT YOU WANT TO SAY. THERE ARE NO OUTSIDERS HERE.

PARDON ME, BUT YOU MAY BE MISTAKEN. RAGHOBADADA PESHWA IS APPROACHING INDORE WITH A BIG ARMY. ONE OF OUR OWN MEN HAS CALLED HIM.

REALLY! WHO IS HE? HOW CAN YOU ACCUSE ANYBODY WITHOUT PROOF?

THE MESSENGER HESITATED.

20

WHEN TUKOJI CAME—

TUKOJI, YOU ARE MY ABLE LIEUTENANT. RAGHOBA WANTS TO PLAY MISCHIEF. GET OUR ARMY READY.

TAKE THESE MESSAGES TO THE PESHWA MADHAVRAO IN POONA AND TO OUR FRIENDS IN GWALIOR, NAGPUR, BARODA...

AT THE COURT OF MADHAVRAO PESHWA—

WRITE TO AHILYABAI THAT WE DISAPPROVE OF RAGHOBA'S ACTION. LET HER PUNISH ALL WHO COME IN HER WAY.

WHEN THE MESSAGE REACHED AHILYABAI AT INDORE—

* SHRIMANT HAS GIVEN US HIS FULL SUPPORT. NOW WE MAY FIGHT FOR WHAT IS RIGHTFULLY OURS.

* THE PESHWA.

21

AT UJJAIN, ON THE BANKS OF THE KSHIPRA—

THAT IS QUITE AN ARMY.

SARKAR, RAGHOBA'S ARMY IS REPORTED TO BE 50,000 STRONG.

SUDDENLY—

SARKAR, WE FOUND HIM HIDING BEHIND THE TENT. HE IS FROM THE PESHWA'S ARMY.

SET HIM FREE. GO BACK AND TELL RAGHOBA THAT IF HE AND HIS ARMY CROSS THE KSHIPRA, IT WILL MEAN WAR.

IN RAGHOBA'S CAMP—

SO THAT'S WHAT TUKOJI SAYS, DOES HE? HE WILL LEARN...

WHAT'S THE NOISE OUTSIDE?

SARKAR, A MESSENGER HAS COME FROM AHILYABAI.

BRING HIM IN.

I HAVE BROUGHT A LETTER FOR YOUR HONOUR.

"...I AM PREPARED TO FIGHT YOUR ARMY. PLEASE REMEMBER, HOWEVER, THAT IF I LOSE, NOBODY WILL TAKE ANY NOTICE. BUT IF YOU LOSE AT THE HANDS OF A MERE WOMAN... CONSIDER THE CONSEQUENCES..."

H'MM... I SEE!

NONSENSE! WHO TOLD AHILYADEVI WE HAVE COME TO FIGHT? GO TELL HER THAT WE HAVE COME TO PAY A VISIT BECAUSE OF HER SON'S DEATH.

THE MESSENGER CAME BACK TO AHILYA'S COURT—

OH, I DIDN'T KNOW THAT IT WAS A PESHWA CUSTOM TO PAY A CONDOLENCE VISIT WITH A 50,000-STRONG ARMY.

AHILYA THUS DEFEATED RAGHOBA BY HER CLEVERNESS.

IN 1766, AHILYABAI SHIFTED HER CAPITAL FROM INDORE TO MAHESHWAR.

AHILYABAI BUILT AND RENOVATED MANY TEMPLES IN MAHESHWAR, STARTED SANSKRIT SCHOOLS, ENCOURAGED THE ANCIENT ART OF WEAVING, REVIVED THE FAMOUS MAHESHWARI SARIS...

WHILE PEACE REIGNED EVERYWHERE, THERE WERE MINOR DISTURBANCES.

THEY HAVE CUT AND TAKEN MY HARVEST AWAY IN ONE NIGHT!

ALL MY CASH WAS ROBBED WHILE I WAS TRAVELLING.

DACOITS WERE HARASSING PEOPLE. MANY COMPLAINTS WERE COMING IN EVERY DAY.

WHAT IS TO BE DONE? HOW CAN I FIND A MAN WHO CAN TACKLE THIS NUISANCE...OH, I HAVE AN IDEA.

27

I WILL DO IT. I WILL NEED SOME MONEY AND CO-OPERATION FROM OUR ARMY.

THE YOUNG MAN, YASHWANTRAO PHANSE, SUCCEEDED IN DEFEATING THE DACOITS.

MUKTABAI WAS MARRIED TO YASHWANTRAO, A BRAVE BUT POOR MAN. AHILYA BROKE ANOTHER TRADITION – PRINCESSES ONLY MARRIED PRINCES.

ABOUT THIS TIME, THE RAJPUTS FROM THE NEIGHBOURING KINGDOM STARTED HARASSING AHILYA'S SUBJECTS.

YOU ARE RULED BY A WOMAN! SHAME! LOOK AT OUR RULERS – THE BRAVE RAJPUTS –THE CHANDRAVATS.

BRING OUT YOUR ORNAMENTS AND YOUR CASH. PAY YOUR RESPECTS TO THE CHANDRAVATS.

THEY HAVE BEEN GOING TO ALL THE VILLAGES. IT MUST BE STOPPED.

AHILYA'S CLEVERNESS AT WINNING BATTLES WITHOUT GOING TO THE BATTLEFIELD WAS SEEN AGAIN IN THE REVOLT OF THE CHANDRAVATS. SHE GAVE THEM 31 TOWNS IN EXCHANGE FOR PEACE.

AFTER SOME TIME, THE CHANDRAVATS AGAIN CAME WITH A BIG ARMY.

TUKOJI WAS AWAY WITH THE HOLKAR ARMY FIGHTING IN THE NORTH.

30

AHILYA ASSUMED THE COMMAND OF THE ARMY AND MARCHED AGAINST THE CHANDRAVATS.

THE BATTLE WAS FIERCE. AHILYA'S ARMY WAS VERY SMALL.

BUT THE HOLKAR ARMY CAME HOME VICTORIOUS.

AHILYABAI LIVED TO A RIPE OLD AGE. HER WORK IS REMEMBERED TO THIS DAY. IN MANY PARTS OF INDIA, YOU WILL FIND MONUMENTS TO AHILYA'S GENEROSITY AND PIOUSNESS.

SUBSCRIBE NOW!

Pay only ₹~~1080~~ **800!**

25% OFF

A twelve month subscription to **TINKLE** and **TINKLE DIGEST**

YOUR DETAILS*

Student's Name _____

Parent's Name _____

Date of Birth: _____ (DD MM YYYY)

Address: _____

_____

_____

City: _____ PIN: _____

State: _____

School: _____

Class: _____

Email (Student): _____

Email (Parent): _____

Tel of Parent: (R): _____

Mobile: _____

_____
Parent's Signature:

*All the above fields are mandatory for the subscription to get activated.

PAYMENT OPTIONS

☐ **Credit Card**
Card Type: Visa ☐ MasterCard ☐
Please charge ₹800 to my Credit Card Number
below:☐☐☐☐ ☐☐☐☐ ☐☐☐☐ ☐☐☐☐
Expiry Date: ☐☐ ☐☐

Cardmember's Signature:

☐ **CHEQUE / DD**
Enclosed please find cheque / DD no. ☐☐☐☐☐☐ drawn
favour of "ACK Media Direct Pvt. Ltd."
on (bank) _____,
for the amount _____, dated ☐☐/☐☐/☐☐☐☐an
send it to: **IBH magazine Service, Arch no.30, Below
Mahalaxmi Bridge, Near Racecourse, Mahalaxmi,
Mumbai 400034**

☐ **Pay by VPP**
Please pay the ₹800 to the postman on the delivery
of 1st issue. (Additional charges ₹30 apply)

☐ **Online subscription**
Visit www.amarchitrakatha.com

For any queries or further information please
write to us ACK Media Direct Pvt. Ltd.,
Krishna House, 3rd Floor, Raghuvanshi Mills Compund,
Senapati Bapat Marg, Lower Parel, Mumbai 400 013.
Tel: 022-40 49 74 36
or send us an Email at customercare@ack-media.com